C
D0209470

Dear mouse friends,
Welcome to the world of

Geronimo Stilton

NO LONGER PROPERTY OF
SEATTLE PUBLIC LIBRARY

THE RODENT'S GAZETTE
EDITORIAL STAFF

Geronimo Stilton
A learned and brainy mouse; editor of *The Rodent's Gazette*

Thea Stilton
Geronimo's sister and special correspondent at *The Rodent's Gazette*

Trap Stilton
An awful joker; Geronimo's cousin and owner of the store Cheap Junk for Less

Benjamin Stilton
A sweet and loving nine-year-old mouse; Geronimo's favorite nephew

Geronimo Stilton

THE HUNT FOR THE HUNDREDTH KEY

PLUS a bonus Mini Mystery and cheesy jokes!

Scholastic Inc.

Pages i–111; 194–214 copyright © 2017 by Edizioni Piemme S.p.A., Palazzo Mondadori, Via Mondadori 1, 20090 Segrate, Italy.

Pages 112–193 copyright © 2008 by Edizioni Piemme S.p.A.

International Rights © Atlantyca S.p.A.

Pages i–111; 194–214 English translation © 2017 by Atlantyca S.p.A.

Pages 112–193 English translation © 2014 by Atlantyca S.p.A.

The publisher does not have any control over and does not assume any responsibility for author or third-party websites or their content.

GERONIMO STILTON names, characters, and related indicia are copyright, trademark, and exclusive license of Atlantyca S.p.A. All rights reserved. The moral right of the author has been asserted. Based on an original idea by Elisabetta Dami. www.geronimostilton.com

Published by Scholastic Inc., *Publishers since 1920*, 557 Broadway, New York, NY 10012. SCHOLASTIC and associated logos are trademarks and/or registered trademarks of Scholastic Inc.

Stilton is the name of a famous English cheese. It is a registered trademark of the Stilton Cheese Makers' Association. For more information, go to www.stiltoncheese.com.

No part of this publication may be reproduced, stored in a retrieval system, or transmitted in any form or by any means, electronic, mechanical, photocopying, recording, or otherwise, without written permission from the copyright holder. For information regarding permission, please contact: Atlantyca S.p.A., Via Leopardi 8, 20123 Milan, Italy; e-mail foreignrights@atlantyca.it, www.atlantyca.com.

This book is a work of fiction. Names, characters, places, and incidents are either the product of the author's imagination or are used fictitiously, and any resemblance to actual persons, living or dead, business establishments, events, or locales is entirely coincidental.

ISBN 978-1-338-08778-9

Pages i–111
Text by Geronimo Stilton
Original title *Il Castello delle 100 Storie*
Cover by Danilo Barozzi
Illustrations by Alessandro Muscillo (design) and Christian Aliprandi (color)
Graphics by Michela Battaglin

Pages 112–193
Text by Geronimo Stilton
Original title *La doppia ladra*
Illustrations by Elena Tomasutti (pencils and ink) and Davide Turotti (color)
Graphics by Michela Battaglin and Marta Lorini
Fingerprint graphic © NREY/Shutterstock

Special thanks to AnnMarie Anderson and Kathryn Cristaldi
Translated by Anna Pizzelli and Andrea Schaffer
Interior design by Becky James

10 9 8 7 6 5 4 3 2 1 17 18 19 20 21

Printed in Malaysia 108
First edition, April 2017

TABLE OF CONTENTS

The Hunt for
the Hundredth Key 1

Mini Mystery:
The Double Cross 111

Geronimo's Jokes 194

THE HUNT FOR THE HUNDREDTH KEY

A Very Special Request

It was **nighttime** in New Mouse City. Rodents everywhere were sound asleep in their beds, snoring peacefully.

Zzz . . . Zzz . . . Zzz . . . Zzz!

I, too, was **cozy** and **warm**, asleep in my little bed.

But at midnight on the dot, my cell phone rang loudly.

RING . . . RING . . . RIIIING!!!

I woke up in a complete **daze** and grabbed my phone.

"Gilton here," I mumbled. "Steronimo Gilton. **Squeak!** I mean Stilton, *Geronimo Stilton*! Who's calling?"

"Grandsonnn!" a voice squeaked shrilly. "I have some **news**! It's very, very **URGENT**! What are you doing, huh? Sleeping?"

I sighed. I recognized that voice. It was my grandfather, **William Shortpaws**. Who else would be calling me in the **middle** of the night? I hoped nothing was wrong at the paper. You see, I am the publisher of *The Rodent's Gazette*, the most famouse newspaper on Mouse Island.

And, unfortunately, my grandfather is the newspaper's founder — and my BOSS!

"Hello, Grandfather," I replied. I knew from experience that I had no choice but to listen. If he had something to say, I was going to HEAR it, one way or another! "Go

ahead: "I'm all ears!"

"The news is that the students at New Mouse City Elementary School have a special request," he squeaked. "They want you to write a new story to help them celebrate the HUNDREDTH day of school. So come on, get out of BED! And don't try to tell me that you're already up, because I know you, Grandson. You're barely awake!"

"Well, yes," I replied, exasperated. "But that's because you called me in the middle of the night!"

"But if I hadn't called you, you'd still be sleeping!" Grandfather replied. "And if you were still sleeping, you wouldn't be

writing. And that's what you need to do right now:

write, write, write!

The hundredth day of school is next week, and the children need that story! And I expect it to be very, very special. It can't just be something to fill up pages. No, it has to be your GREATEST STORY YET! It has to be unique and amazing. In fact, it has to be one in a million!"

Then he hung up on me.

Holey cheese! Why does my grandfather always know just how to get under my fur?

It's true that it was the middle of the NIGHT, but there was no way I would be able to go back to sleep now. I was WIDE AWAKE!

I decided I might as well start writing. You

see, in addition to being publisher at *The Rodent's Gazette*, I'm also an author. And I only had **seven days** to write a brand-new book! Squeak! That's hardly any time at all!

I put on a recording of the New Mouse City Orchestra playing some relaxing instrumental music. Then I sat down at my desk and turned on my computer.

Then I started thinking, and

But I couldn't figure out what to write. This book had to be super special! Thundering cat tails, it was too much **pressure**!

I had a TERRIBLE case of writer's block. What was I going to do?

I thought and thought and thought . . .
and thinking . . .
Argh!

. . . MY LAST TRIP TO TRANSRATANIA?
Hmm, maybe I could write about . . .

. . . OR THE LATEST MYSTERY I SOLVED WITH HERCULE POIRAT?
. . . OR MY TRIP TO THE EGYPTIAN PYRAMIDS?

A Castle in a Faraway Valley

I **thought** and **thought** and **thought**, but I couldn't come up with anything special enough. I couldn't disappoint the children — I had to think of something **amazing**!

Unsure of what to do, I turned off the computer and fixed myself a classic MIDNIGHT SNACK:

a cup of hot chocolate . . .

A SLICE OF BLUE CHEESE PIE . . .

and a mozzarella smoothie!

But just as I was about to sit down to eat, my cell phone rang again. Cheese and crackers! Could it be Grandfather again?

I answered the **phone**, and it was my sister, Thea.

"Hi, G, it's me!" she squeaked excitedly. "Turn on the TV **right away**. I'm going to be on Trap's show *Chasing Secrets* on **MYSTERY MOUSE TV** tonight!"

I hurried to the living room and turned on the TV. The show was about to start.

MYSTERY MOUSE TV PRESENTS

CHASING SECRETS

hosted by **TRAP STILTON**

In this new show, Trap Stilton uncovers the secrets of Mouse Island! Join Trap as he explores the mysterious Smelly Cave and takes you on an expedition to the Hamster Islands. You will be shocked and amazed at the many secrets he reveals!

Have you heard of *Chasing Secrets*? It's the top-rated show on Mystery Mouse TV, and my cousin **Trap Stilton** happens to be the host. He talks about **ANYTHING** and **EVERYTHING** that's mysterious on Mouse Island!

"Dear rodent viewers," Trap began, "I have some exciting news to report. A mysterious castle has been discovered in a faraway, forgotten valley. An impervious forest of thorny bushes has hidden this castle from view for many years. But now our very own adventurous special correspondent,

THEA STILTON

FIRST NAME: Thea
LAST NAME: Stilton
WHO SHE IS: Geronimo Stilton's sister
OCCUPATION: Special correspondent for *The Rodent's Gazette*, the most famouse newspaper on Mouse Island. She is also special correspondent for the Mystery Mouse TV show *Chasing Secrets*, which is directed by her cousin Trap.
HER SECRET: She is always well-informed, and she never misses out on a scoop!

THEA STILTON, has made an amazing discovery!"

The AUDIENCE burst into applause.

CLAP! CLAP! CLAP!

"And now, here is THEA STILTON!" Trap exclaimed.

At that moment, my sister's snout appeared on the screen.

"As you all know, our beloved *New Mouse City* was founded by the legendary **Grant**

Gentlemouse," Thea said. "One of the many **legends** about Grant Gentlemouse is that he had a **mysterious** castle built for his beloved bride. The castle was supposedly very tall, with **golden** towers. It was built out of **IVORY-COLORED** marble, and it is decorated with hundreds of **beautiful** roses! According to this legend, it was called the **Castle of One Hundred Stories**. Now, for the first time, I have an exclusive special investigation on this legendary castle! And it's only here on

MYSTERY MOUSE TV!"

MYSTERY MOUSE TV

Thea pointed to a video screen behind her in the TV studio.

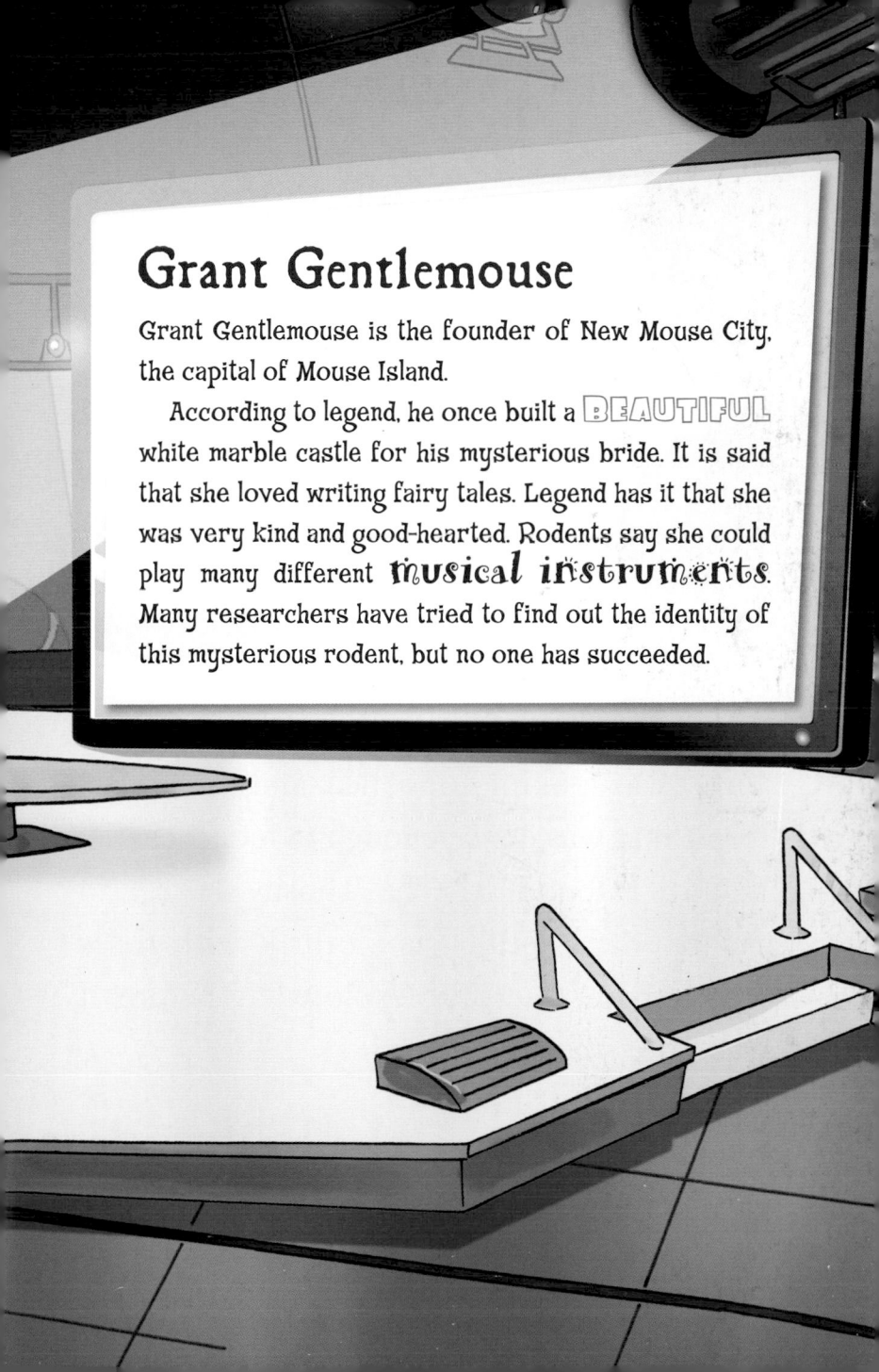

Grant Gentlemouse

Grant Gentlemouse is the founder of New Mouse City, the capital of Mouse Island.

According to legend, he once built a BEAUTIFUL white marble castle for his mysterious bride. It is said that she loved writing fairy tales. Legend has it that she was very kind and good-hearted. Rodents say she could play many different **musical instruments**. Many researchers have tried to find out the identity of this mysterious rodent, but no one has succeeded.

"Here is how I rediscovered the location of this fabumouse castle:

"First, I **studied** all the documents I could find that mentioned the **Castle of the Hundred Stories**.

"Next, I spent **months** in my airplane, flying over the land around New Mouse City. I was looking for a **TALL** and **twisted** forest that was dense enough to hide a castle. Finally, I found it! The Thorny Forest in **Roseland County** is so thick with roses that nobody has ever explored it before. I was sure the **Castle of One Hundred Stories** was hidden there.

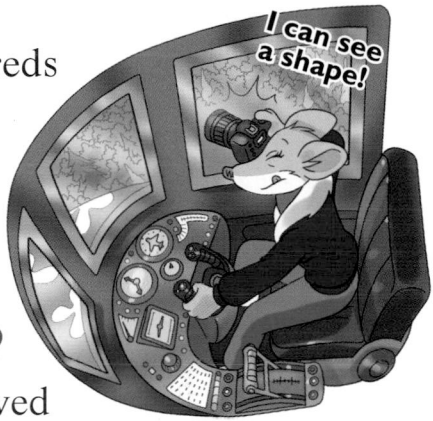

"Then, I took hundreds of **photographs** of the forest from the airplane. I noticed that one area of the forest was **darker** than the rest when viewed from above.

"Finally, I analyzed the photographs on my **computer** and was amazed to find that the dark area of the forest took the shape of a **CASTLE**! I can now confirm it: A mysterious castle is hidden in the forest, and I am positive it is the legendary **Castle of One Hundred Stories**!"

Roseland County is one of the most mysterious areas on Mouse Island. The thick bushes of thorny white roses that grow there make the forest incredibly dense and difficult to explore. The rodents that live there use its amazing roses in many different ways: They build furniture using the wood from the branches, they spin fabric from the roots, and they cook special dishes from the flowers and leaves . . .

ROSE SOUP
WITH HOT PEPPERS

ROSE-LEAF
POT PIE

ROSE AND
RICOTTA RAVIOLI

ROSE LASAGNA

BREADED, DEEP-
FRIED ROSES

ROSE-LEAF TEA
WITH LEMON

CHEWY ROSE
CARAMELS

ROSE ICE CREAM

SWEET ROSE JAM

CRISPY CHEDDAR
ROSE COOKIES

ROSE-FILLED
CHOCOLATE
TRUFFLES

ROSE LEAF-
INFUSED COFFEE

A Mysterious, Dangerous Adventure

My cousin Trap appeared on the TV SCREEN, a mischievous look on his snout.

"That sounds SOOOOOO interesting," he exclaimed. "What will you do next, Thea?"

"Well, there's only one thing to do now," she replied excitedly. "I will go to Roseland County

right away to explore the Thorny Forest and try to find the mysterious **Castle of One Hundred Stories**!"

"Let's go!" Trap squeaked impatiently.

But Thea had a serious look on her snout.

"I have to warn you, Trap," she explained. "There is a reason no one has ever explored the Thorny Forest before! It is home to thousands of **Thorny Thornix** roses, which only grow in Roseland County. They're twice as BIG as normal roses and three times as fragrant. But their thorns are as POINTY as knives, as **SHARP** as razors, and as **STRONG** as steel! In other words, venturing into the Thorny Forest is extremely **DANGEROUS**!"

"Yes!" Trap squeaked. "I love a **mysterious**, **DANGEROUS** adventure!"

Thea nodded. "At this point, we could really use an **assistant** to help us out,"

she said. "Someone to carry the backpacks, prepare breakfast, and **fund** our trip. After all, it's going to be very, very **expensive**! And I have the perfect mouse in mind."

"Well, hurry up and tell our viewers who it is!" Trap replied, an eager glint in his eye.

Thea turned to the audience, a huge **GRIN** on her snout.

"It's none other than my fabumouse brother, Geronimo Stilton!" she squeaked. "And I'll call him **right now** to tell him!"

"Stilton?!" the audience **shouted**. "*Geronimo Stilton*? The publisher of *The Rodent's Gazette*? **YAYYYYY!**"

But Trap seemed less **enthusiastic**.

"Hmmm," he said. "Are you sure? I mean, he's a bit of a scaredy-mouse . . ."

But Thea just shook her snout.

"Geronimo will be part of the TEAM!" she replied.

Trap turned to the camera.

"You heard her, dear viewers," he said smoothly. "We are about to leave on this expensive, adventurous, and **dangerous** expedition. Thea will be the special correspondent, Geronimo will be the assistant, and I will **FILM** everything live for you! It will be the most fabumouse episode of *Chasing Secrets* yet!"

My whiskers **trembled**. What in the

name of cheese were they talking about? I absolutely was not going on a mysterious, dangerous, adventurous, and, above all, very, very expensive trip. **NO WAY!**

Right then, my telephone rang again.

"Uh, Stilton here," I squeaked.

"We're picking you up in **ten minutes**, so start packing," my sister shouted. "It's going to be fabumouse!"

CLICK!

My sister had already **HUNG UP** on me. **Rotten ricotta!** What was I going to do?

Through the Thorny Maze

Less than ten minutes later, my sister's **Hot-Pink** SUV ***screeched*** to a stop in front of my house. Trap was with her.

I had to put my paw down. There was **no way** I was going with them!

"I'm sorry, Thea," I began, "but I can't

leave! I have to write a —"

"Save it, G," Thea cut me off as Trap PUSHED me toward the car. "You're coming with us, and that's FINAL!"

"Yup," Trap agreed. Then he reached into my pocket and pulled out my MASTER MOUSE credit card. "We need you . . . and your MONEY!"

Before I could squeak "Cheese niblets," I was in the car and we were ***zooming*** toward Roseland County and the Thorny Forest.

The Thorny Forest was so DENSE, we

Start
Which route should they take to reach the Castle of One Hundred Stories?

THE SOLUTION IS ON PAGE 110.

were sure to get lost. I was so worried!

But my sister and my cousin didn't seem to have a care in the world. We just sped past one thorny bush after another, going around and around and around in circles. Pretty soon, we were completely lost!

Then a heavy FOG descended on the forest, making it look even spookier!

I WAS INCREDIBLY NERVOUS!

As if that wasn't enough, a storm was

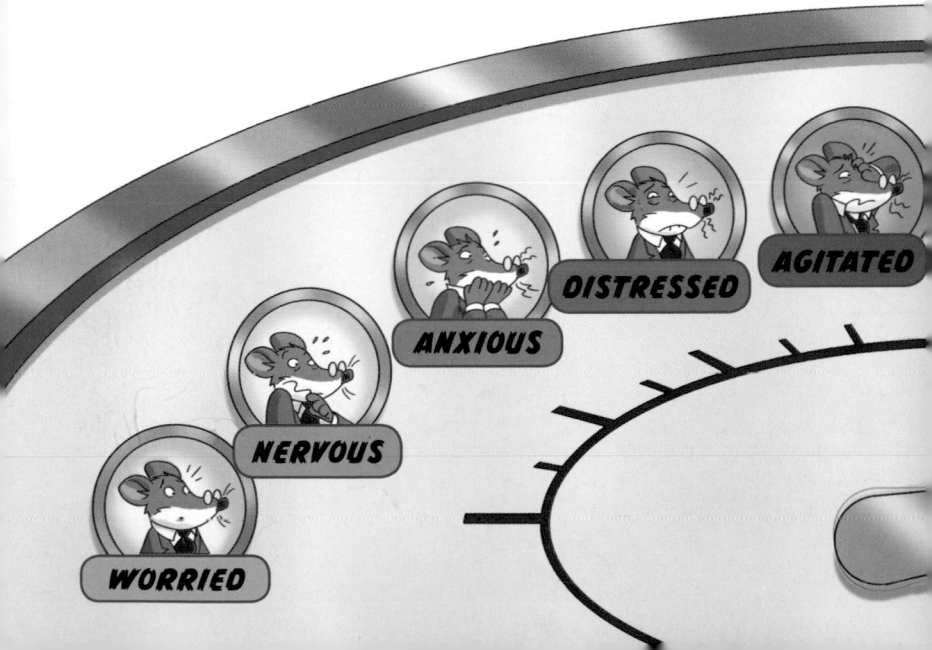

LOOMING. The sky crackled with lightning. *I was beyond scared!*

Suddenly, we heard some howling in the distance.

"Hmm," Thea said. "Must be wolves . . . Hope they're not too HUNGRY!"

NOW I WAS ABSOLUTELY TERRIFIED! *Rat-munching rattlesnakes!* Why, oh, why hadn't I stayed home?

A moment later, we saw tons of pairs of

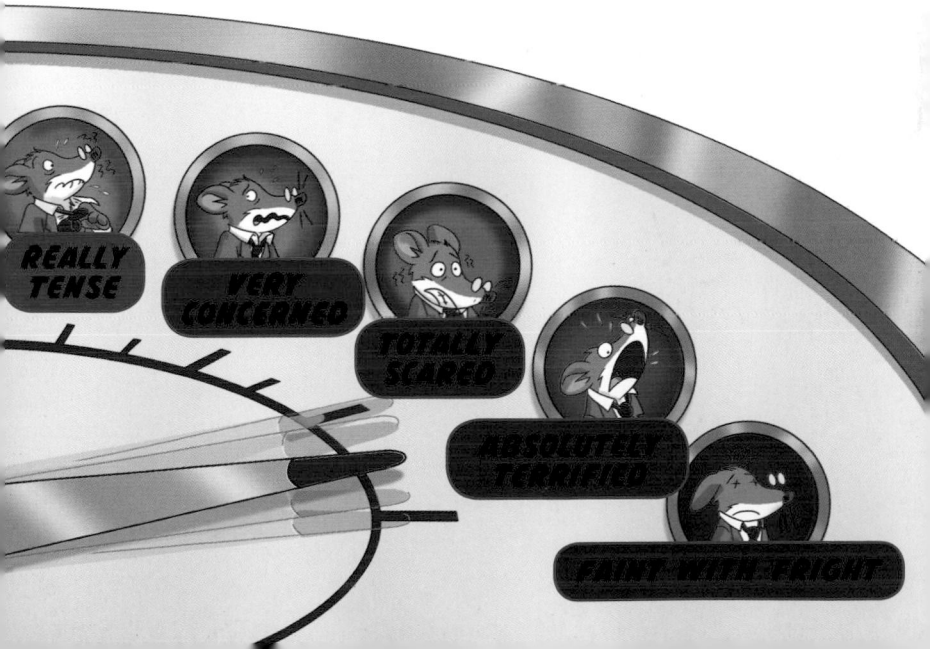

yellow EYES staring at us through the forest. Squeak! It was the wolves! I fainted.

Suddenly, I felt COLD water on my snout.

"Wake up!" Trap shouted. He had dumped an entire bucket of water over my head.

For some reason, the wolves decided to leave us alone. Maybe they didn't like the taste of mouse! We continued to drive slowly through the DARK and foggy forest. Eventually, we came to a golden gate with the initials "R.S." on it.

Whose initials were they?

We went through the gate and entered what was once a huge formal garden. We continued down a dark road lined with statues.

At the end of the road, we came to a tall, majestic castle made of ivory marble with a golden rooftop.

Thea leaped out of the car and began running toward the castle.

"It's here!" she squeaked joyfully. "It's really here! HOW EXCITING!"

Trap jumped out of the car, too.

"I've got to get this on film!" he cried.

I looked out at the dark castle LOOMING above me. Squeak! HOW SCARY! But then I thought about what it would be like to sit in the car all alone with the wolves circling around me.

"Hey!" I shouted. "Wait for meeeeeeeee!

Don't leave me here by myself!"

At that moment, a bolt of **LIGHTNING** hit the tallest tower of the castle.

"**HEEEEEEEEEEEK!**" I screamed, my whiskers shaking with fear.

Meanwhile, Thea was snapping photos.

"Wow!" she cried. "I got an amazing shot just as the lightning hit the tower. **HOW SPOOKY!**"

"Geronimo!" Trap shouted. "Hurry up with that equipment! This storm is setting the perfect mysterious mood for my show, and I'm missing it!"

I'm so scared!
We're rolling!
What a shot!

A Heart-Shaped Stone

We **scampered** over the drawbridge and across the castle's **deep** moat. When we reached the front entrance, Thea shined her flashlight at the top of the enormouse **STONE DOORS**.

"Look up there!" she squeaked. We looked up to see a **heart-shaped** marble stone with an **INSCRIPTION** that had faded with time.

We tried to make out the entire **inscription**, but the **THICK FOG** and the faded letters didn't help.

"Then it's true!" Thea

THIS CASTLE IS BUILT
FOR MY BELOVED BRIDE
GRAST
GENTLEMOUSE
Look up there!

squeaked happily. "This is the castle Grant Gentlemouse built for his bride. I was right! But we still don't know her name."

"Wait a second," Trap said as he switched on his camera. "I have to get this IMPORTANT DISCOVERY on film! Three . . . two . . . one . . . ACTION!"

Thea turned on the charm as she grabbed the microphone.

"Rodents of Mouse Island, I am proud to announce an amazing DISCOVERY," she squeaked. "We have found **Grant Gentlemouse's** legendary castle! I can also confirm that it was indeed built for his beloved bride."

Thea gestured toward the carving above the doors. "We don't know her name yet, but we hope to soon find out the identity of this mysterious rodent. Now come along as we enter the castle and uncover the answers to many more mysteries. Our **ADVENTURE** is just beginning!"

Trap gave my sister a big paws-up. Then he turned off his camera, and the three of us prepared to enter the **ancient** castle.

How Scared Are You, from One to Ten?

We stood in front of the main door to the castle. It was very **TALL** and made of solid oak, with a bronze **DOOR KNOCKER** in the shape of a rose. At one time, the door must have been incredibly **beautiful**. But years of wind, rain, and neglect had **weathered** the wood. Now it was dry and brittle. As soon as Thea pushed the door, it opened with a **SPOOKY** creaking sound.

YIKES! HOW SCARY!

As soon as I walked in, I realized the **castle** must have been truly **splendid** in the past. The ceilings were made of ivory marble and **DECORATED** with precious **gold** molding. And the chandeliers and candelabras were made of solid **brass**.

The **BOOKCASES** were filled with antique books, and the walls were covered with fancy wallpaper that was **embroidered** with a

How beautiful!
Wow!
Amazing!

rose petal design. The velvet curtains were decorated with **small** roses that had been sewn on with golden thread.

But everything was covered in a **thick** layer of dust, and there were enormouse SPIDERWEBS in every corner. It was clear the castle had been DESERTED for a very long time. It was old and in need of a good RENOVATION!

"Well, what are we waiting for?" Thea said impatiently. "Let's start exploring!"

I flicked on my FLASHLIGHT, but Trap stopped me.

"Put that away," he said. "It will look much more **mysterious** for the cameras if we explore using candlelight!"

He shoved a **brass** candlestick holder into my paw and LIT the candles. A spooky **SHADOW** projected on the walls. I knew

it was my own shadow, but I still JUMPED about three feet!

Squeak! It looked like a scary cat!

SQUEAK! A SCARY CAT!

Meanwhile, Trap made up a little song for the camera as he poked around.

"Creepy shadows, moldy rooms,
This old place is full of gloom!
Spiderwebs in every nook,
Drafty windows, dusty books!
Come on and explore with me—
We'll solve this creepy mystery!"

"And now I have an exclusive interview with my scaredy-mouse cousin, Geronimo Stilton!" Trap said. Then he thrust the **microphone** under my snout.

"Tell our viewers: How does it feel to explore a mysterious, creepy, **abandoned** castle like this one, huh? A castle that's full of cobwebs and that might even be **haunted**?"

"Um, it's r-really e-exciting," I stammered nervously, my teeth **chattering** in fright.

Trap laughed and started singing again:

"Chattering teeth, lots of fear!
Castle spooks, far and near.
So many secrets hide inside,
Like the name of old Grant's bride!"

Then he turned his camera on me once more.

"You're scared, aren't you, Geronimo?" he snickered. "Tell our viewers: How scared are you now, from one to ten? From the look of your PALE snout, I would say it's at least a **nine**!"

Before I could even reply, he started telling SPOOKY jokes to scare me even more . . .

SPOOKY JOKES

Q: What did the street sign in the cemetery say?

A: Dead end!

First mouse: Knock, knock!

Second mouse: Who's there?

First mouse: Ice cream!

Second mouse: Ice cream who?

First mouse: *I scream* every time I see a ghost!

Q: What's the first thing a vampire learns in school?

A: The alpha*bat*!

Q: Where does a vampire eat his lunch?

A: In the *casketeria*!

Q: What's a mummy's favorite music?

A: *Wrap* music!

Overheard between two ghosts:

"Do you feel like going with me to the graveyard?"

"Sure, I'm dying to!"

THE GOLDEN KEYS

While Trap was busy trying to scare me out of my fur, my sister was poking around in dusty corners. Eventually, Trap ran out of jokes, and Thea called us over.

"Geronimo! Trap!" she squeaked. "Come here — quick! Look at this."

I raised my candlestick and ILLUMINATED the wall in front of us. An enormouse key ring with tons of solid GOLD KEYS hung on a hook. A poem was inscribed in the wall right above the keys.

It was some sort of riddle! As soon as Trap **read** the word *treasure*, his eyes grew as **LARGE** as wheels of cheese.

"Treasure?" he squeaked. "This **mysterious**

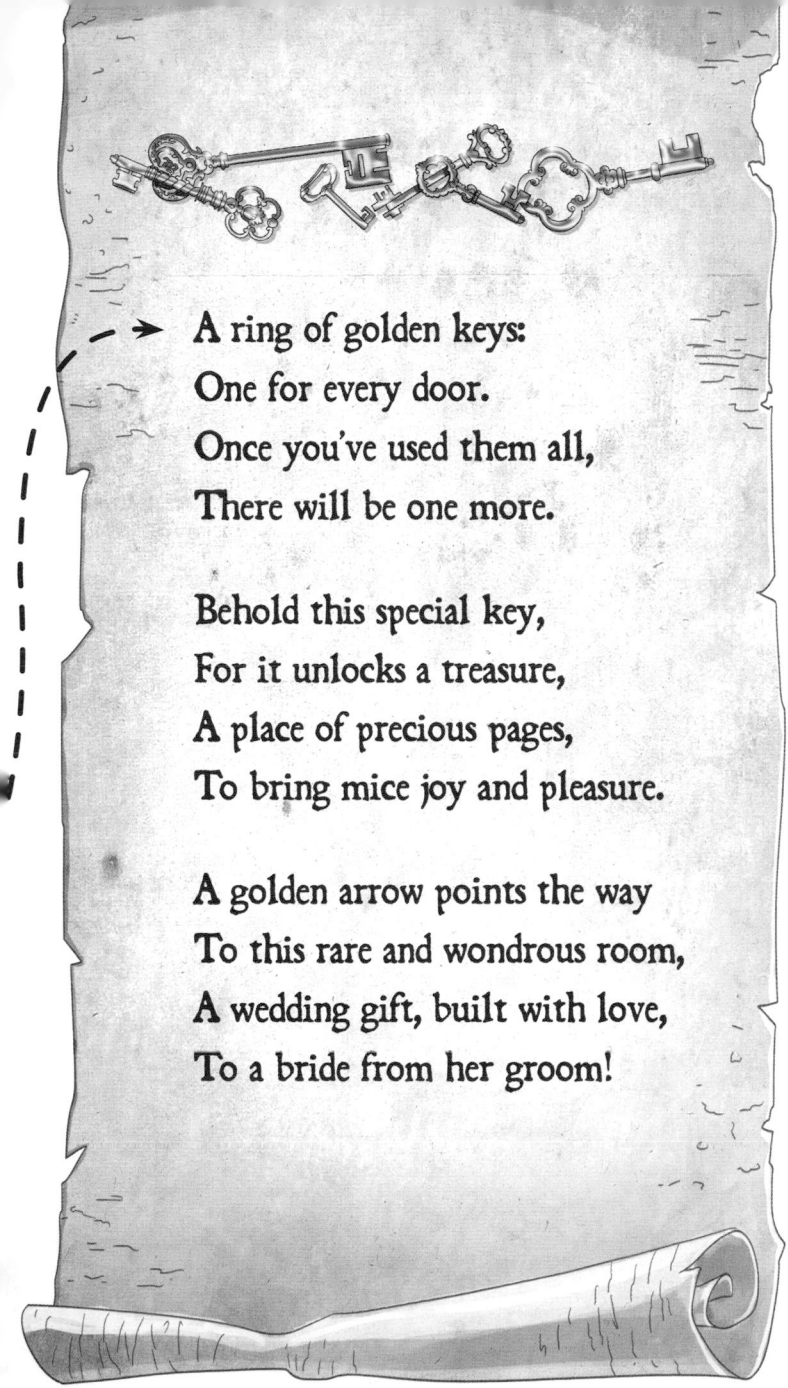

A ring of golden keys:
One for every door.
Once you've used them all,
There will be one more.

Behold this special key,
For it unlocks a treasure,
A place of precious pages,
To bring mice joy and pleasure.

A golden arrow points the way
To this rare and wondrous room,
A wedding gift, built with love,
To a bride from her groom!

Which key matches

THE SOLUTION IS ON PAGE 110.

the white shape?

castle is getting better by the second!"

Thea was intent on solving the riddle, too.

"Hmmm . . . I wonder what 'a place of precious pages' could be," she murmured. "And a golden arrow? How strange! I can't seem to figure it out. There's only one

thing to do — let's start exploring!"

Thea put all the keys on a **silver** tray and pawed it to me. Then she grabbed the **CANDLESTICK** and headed up the stairs.

"Have you two been **MUMMIFIED**? What are you waiting for?" she scolded. "Let's go!"

When we reached the top of the stairs, we found ourselves in a **HALLWAY** lined with many doors.

Thea stopped in front of the first door, handed me the candlestick, and took a KEY from the tray. She put it in the **keyhole**, but it didn't UNLOCK the door.

Then she tried ANOTHER KEY, and ANOTHER, and ANOTHER, and ANOTHER, until the door finally opened. But there was NOTHING inside!

Thea moved on to the second door, and the third one after that. It took forever to find the right key each time. We opened DOOR after DOOR after DOOR until we couldn't keep track of where we had been anymore.

THE MYSTERIOUS KEY

Most of the rooms were empty. But in one room, we found a collection of **antique armor**.

As I was studying a unique sword, I heard a squeaking sound behind me. I turned to find that one of the suits of armor had come to **life** and was lumbering toward me!

"**I'M COMING FOR YOUR TAIL!**" the suit howled.

"HEEELP!" I squeaked, scared out of my fur. "A ghost!"

But the suit of armor just burst out laughing.

"Ha, ha, ha!" Trap giggled from inside. "It's only me, Cuz!"

Next we entered the castle's kitchen. A trail of mysterious white pawprints stretched across the floor.

"Squeak!" I gasped. "It's really a ghost this time!"

Again, Trap laughed.

"You're such a scaredy-

mouse, G," he said. "There's no such thing as a ghost!"

Then we **walked** into the library. Inside, we found a door that led to a small, SECRET courtyard. There we opened a heart-shaped gate and ended up in an incredible ROSE GARDEN filled with a thousand fragrant flowering white roses.

"Wow!" Thea squeaked. "What a fabumouse place!"

Finally, we walked through the enormouse dance hall and ended up in the throne room. There were two THRONES: one

for Grant Gentlemouse and one for his mysterious bride.
But once again, we couldn't read her name!
From the throne room, we found another KEY that unlocked a door leading to the
Still no name!

TALLEST tower in the castle and the bride's private rooms.

Inside, we found a closet full of stunning SILK dresses and a collection of colorful shoes. But there was still **no name**!

From there, yet another KEY opened the door to the cellar. It was so DAMP and DARK down there! Suddenly, I felt a cold breath on my neck.

"Chattering cheddar, there's a ghost!" I squeaked at the top of my lungs.

Trap snickered. He was BLOWING air on my neck with a bellows. Why does my cousin have to be such a prankster?

After searching the whole castle and

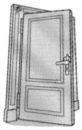

opening **NINETY-NINE** doors, one last MYSTERIOUS KEY was left on the silver tray.

It was engraved with golden roses and the letters R.S.

"If there is a **HUNDREDTH** key, there must be a **HUNDREDTH** door!" Thea said excitedly.

This key
will open the
hundredth door!

I peered out the window. It was almost daylight. Suddenly, the curtain next to me fluttered. Then it reached out and grabbed me.

"Moldy mozzarella!" I shrieked. "It's a ghost for sure! This castle really *is* haunted!"

Then Trap popped out from behind the curtain, laughing.

"Don't be silly, Geronimo," he teased. "I was just pulling your tail."

We continued searching the castle for the hundredth room. We even knocked on walls,

looking for a hollow spot that might reveal a **hidden** entrance.

But we found **NOTHING**!

We checked every **BOOKCASE** for a secret hidden switch that would spin the bookcase around, revealing a hidden door.

But we found **NOTHING**!

We moved all the furniture to see if anything was covering the hundredth door. But we

found NOTHING!

Then I realized I really had to use the restroom!

I opened a door and entered a GLOOMY black marble bathroom. Suddenly, I saw a SHADOWY figure in the corner.

"HELP!" I squeaked. "GHOST IN THE GARDEROBE!"

Then I fainted.

When I came to, Trap was doubled over with laughter.

"What in the name of cheese is a garderobe?" he asked between giggles.

I stood up and tried to look dignified.

"It's the name for a bathroom in a medieval castle," I explained. And for once in his life, my cousin was squeakless!

It didn't last long, though.

"You're a real smarty-mouse, Cuz," Trap said, chuckling. Then he raised his right paw. "Tell you what? I'll give you a BREAK. No more breathing on your neck, wrapping you up in curtains, or HOWLING like a ghost. Mouse's honor!"

We shook paws in agreement and began searching for the hundredth room again. But a second later, a huge SHADOW flitted across the wall.

"HELP!" I squeaked. "A WITCH!"

Again, Trap doubled over laughing.

"I promised no more ghosts, but I didn't say anything about SHADOW pranks!"

Shadow Puppets

You can create mouserific shadows using your hands! Try to copy the gestures below. If a light is shining directly on you, a fantastic shadow will appear on the wall.

THE GOLDEN ARROW

Unsure of what to do next, we walked back to the castle's entrance. THEA read the riddle again. Then she was **quiet** for a moment.

"Hmmm," she mumbled. "I just thought of something. The riddle says:

"A golden arrow points the way."

She pointed to a marble **STATUE** of a flying cherub holding a bow. A GOLDEN ARROW was positioned in it. The arrow was aimed at a heart-shaped mirror embellished with roses and engraved with the initials "R.S."

It points to the mirror!
RS

Thea dashed over to the mirror. There we saw a very small **keyhole**. Thea inserted the hundredth key.

I held my **breath**, waiting to see what would happen. Then there was a **soft** *click*, and the mirror **opened** like a door.

Trap **RUSHED** past me, his camera rolling, squeaking at the top of his lungs.

"The mysterious hundredth door! WE FOUND IT!"

I scampered after him. Soon we were in a rose-shaped room lined with shelves.

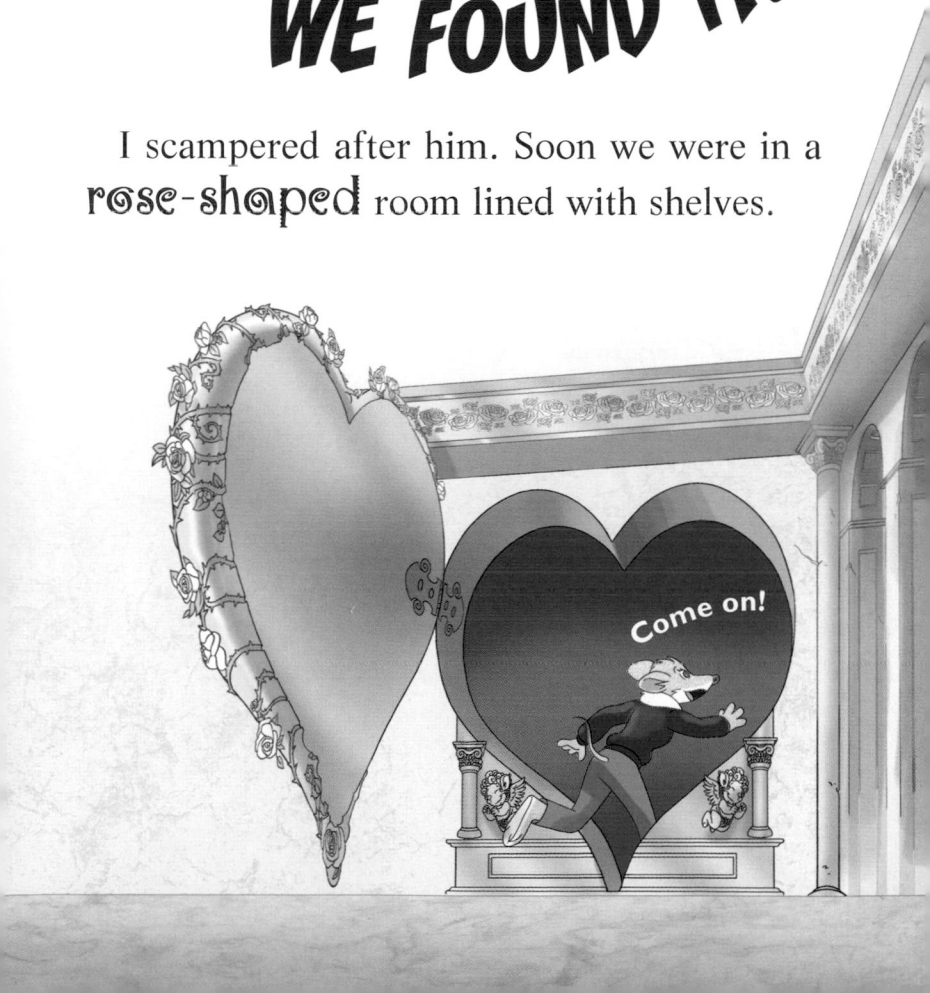

Look!
Wow, what a room!

BEYOND THE MIRROR

I was squeakless. The room was decorated all in WHITE, and the marble floor was etched with a drawing of an enormouse white rose. A small ROSEWOOD desk sat in the center of the room. There was a piece of parchment on top, along with a golden inkwell and a dusty feathered quill.

I stepped closer to see what was written on the parchment. Long ago, someone had written the sentence, "Once upon a time . . ."

That desk had belonged to a writer, just like me!

Once upon a time . . .

I glanced around and noticed that the **WOODEN** shelves lining the walls were divided into compartments. I counted, and there were exactly **one hundred**, just like the **one hundred** rooms in the castle and the **one hundred** keys that opened their doors!

Each shelf contained a rolled manuscript. I pulled out one manuscript after another and realized they were stories! So that's why this was called the **Castle of One Hundred Stories**!

Each story was a beautiful fairy tale, illustrated with amazing **watercolor** paintings. The signature on the illustrations read "R.S." So these stories must have been written and illustrated by **GRANT GENTLEMOUSE'S** mysterious bride!

An Old Portrait of a Mysterious Snout

Trap grabbed the microphone.

"Viewers, we've solved one **mystery**!" he squeaked. "Now we know how the **Castle of One Hundred Stories** got its name! But who is the author of these fairy —"

"Look!" Thea interrupted. "Over there!"

She pointed to a white velvet **curtain** hanging on the wall. It was covering a GOLDEN picture frame.

Thea ran to the curtain and firmly PULLED it aside. She revealed a PORTRAIT of a mouse dressed as a bride! The mysterious mouse was wearing a **silky white** gown embroidered with **golden** roses.

I noticed that the bride's **delicate** gray fur matched the color of my sister's fur **exactly**.

She also had amazing violet eyes, *just like my sister*. Her ears were small and

delicate, *just like my sister's*. She was tall and slim, *just like my sister*.

To make a long story short, she looked like

Thea's twin sister!

Thea **bent down** to examine the bottom edge of the frame. There she uncovered a small GOLDEN plaque with a name engraved on it.

She gasped.

"Oh! It's the mysterious bride's name!"

"**YES!**" Trap squeaked excitedly. "We're going to solve the FINAL MYSTERY! Tell us, Thea: Who was Grant Gentlemouse's bride? Who? Who?"

But Thea was squeakless, her snout as PALE as mozzarella.

"Thea?" I asked. "Tell us the bride's name! We **can't wait** to find out!"

"Yes, tell us!" Trap insisted, waving his microphone under her snout. "The moment is **finally** here!"

THEA TOOK A DEEP BREATH . . .

ONCE UPON A TIME . . .

"The mysterious bride's name is . . . Rose Stilton!" my sister squeaked.

"What?!" Trap and I shouted in unison.

"Stilton?" I asked. "S-T-I-L-T-O-N, Stilton?"

Thea nodded.

"So we're related to Grant Gentlemouse's mysterious bride?" Trap asked.

Thea moved aside so Trap and I could see the plaque up close.

"It's true!" I exclaimed in disbelief. "Her last name is Stilton, just like us. That explains why she looks so much like Thea in the portrait: SHE'S OUR ANCESTOR!"

"Look!" Trap squeaked. He pointed to another curtain.

Her name is Rose Stilton!

Thea pulled it open to reveal a wooden dummy with Rose Stilton's wedding gown, jewelry, and tiara **draped** over it.

Thea slipped on the gown and stood in front of the portrait. The resemblance between her and Rose Stilton was **incredimouse**!

In the meantime, I was busy looking through

the *manuscripts*. Maybe one would explain how we were related to Grant Gentlemouse, the founder of New Mouse City!

When I found the **HUNDREDTH STORY**, I understood . . .

ROSE

Once upon a time, there was a prince named Grant Gentlemouse. He was handsome, strong, and kind, and he loved defending the weakest rodents and protecting the poor. He was nicknamed Grant the Generous because no one who asked for help ever left the castle without something in his or her paws! He fought like a hero, and when he rode up on his white horse, his enemies trembled.

Everyone admired and loved him. When it was time for the rodents of Mouse Island to choose their first governor, they elected Grant Gentlemouse. He wasn't married because he was waiting to meet a mouselet who would steal his heart. One day he met a sweet mouse with a kind heart, and he fell in love.

Her name was Rose Stilton.

They soon got married. And when Gentlemouse founded the first city on

Mouse Island, he made the rose its official flower. To this day, the rose is a special flower to all rodents who live in Mouse Island's capital.

Grant Gentlemouse wanted to give his bride the most beautiful wedding gift imaginable. So he built an ivory marble castle and decorated it with roses everywhere, as a tribute to her. Rose loved to read, so he built a library full of books for her. And since Rose also loved to write, he gave her a beautiful rosewood desk, a gold-and-crystal inkwell engraved with her initials, and one hundred scrolls that she could use to write her stories. These poetic fairy tales fill this room today, to make young and old mice happy.

This is a true story. It is written from Rose's heart as a gift for Grant Gentlemouse, her brave groom!

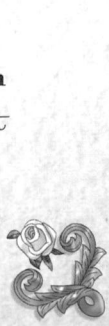

MYSTERIES SOLVED!

By the time I finished reading, I was moved to tears.

"What a beautiful story!" I exclaimed. "This was written centuries ago, but it's still so poignant!"

Thea nodded in agreement, her eyes watery as well. Trap turned OFF the camera with a click, and I was surprised that even he had a little tear on his snout.

"I had no idea where this mystery would lead us!" he said sincerely. "What a fabumouse story of true love!"

Who knew my prankster cousin had a heart as soft as Brie?

But a second later, LOUD, BOSSY Trap was back.

"Thea!" he barked. "Get ready to roll again. Three . . . two . . . one . . . **ACTION**!

"We've solved many **mysteries**!" Trap shouted into his microphone while my sister filmed. "**FIRST**, we found the **Castle of One Hundred Stories**. **SECOND**, we figured out how the castle got its name. **THIRD**, we discovered the name of Grant Gentlemouse's mysterious bride: **Rose Stilton**! And **FINALLY**, we now know why the rose is New Mouse City's **official** flower. Phew!"

Then Trap began jumping **UP** and **DOWN** and singing a victory song.

"Hooray for the Stilton family—
We solved this ancient mystery!
Now we know where the castle hides,
And the name of old Grant's bride.
Rose Stilton is her name;
She will bring our family fame!
In our city her flower blooms,
Thanks to the love of her fair groom!
Hooray for the Stilton family—
We solved this ancient mystery!"

He **pinched** my tail affectionately. "Can you believe it, Cuz?" he asked. "From now on, the *Stilton* family name will be in **history books**!"

With that, we turned off all the cameras, gathered our equipment, and prepared to head home. But first, we walked down the one hundred steps we had climbed up, through the main WOODEN door, and along the path leading toward the garden entrance, where we had parked Thea's SUV.

I looked back at the Castle of One Hundred Stories for a moment. The sun was setting, and the golden roof glittered in the light. We had

How beautiful!
We got some great shots!
What a special story!

only been there for **twenty-four** hours, but I knew I was going to miss that amazing place. I had been so touched by the love story between Grant Gentlemouse and his bride — who was a writer, just like me!

We got back in the car and drove home, leaving the thick **Thorny Forest** behind us. The trip took most of the **NIGHT**. We finally arrived back in New Mouse City at **SUNRISE**.

THE HUNDREDTH DAY STORY

When I got home, I turned on my **computer**. Suddenly, I had a realization: I knew exactly what I would write for the **hundredth day celebration** at New Mouse City Elementary School! I would write the story of the **Castle of One Hundred Stories**.

It would be a great **love** story, and a tale of the **history** of our fair city!

Thanks to my adventure at the castle, I had learned that things that are done in the name of **love** can withstand the test of **time**! That's why I decided to dedicate my new story to that great mouse and author, **Rose Stilton**.

As soon as I finished writing the book, I took it to my **grandfather**. He read it from **BEGINNING** to **END** while I waited anxiously.

WOULD HE LIKE IT?

My whiskers trembled in anticipation.

I was so stressed!

Finally, my grandfather finished reading.

"Grandson," he said sternly. "You finally did something right! We'll publish this book right away, and we'll send copies to all the students at the New Mouse City Elementary School!

I breathed a sigh of relief.

"Terrific!" I said. "Now can I go? I was thinking of taking a little vacation. I'm exhausted after all that writing."

"A vacation?!" Grandfather huffed. "No way, Grandson. It's time to get back to your work as PUBLISHER of *The Rodent's Gazette*! And I'm sure the students at New Mouse City Elementary School will want a **sequel** to this story right away. Your readers always want **more stories**, and we have to make them **happy**!"

He put a 🐾🐾🐾 on my shoulder. "But I know you need a break, so I'll let you take **one day** off before you start writing again!"

ONE DAY? That was nothing! But the more I thought about it, the more I understood.

If my readers wanted more stories, I had to write . . .

write and write and write and write!

Therefore, *dear rodent friends,* I will write as many stories as I can for the students at New Mouse City Elementary

School . . . and for you, my faithful readers! I will write from my **heart** because, thanks to my adventure in the **Castle of One Hundred Stories**, I know that things done in the name of **love** truly have the **power** to last forever!

So I give you my word that there will be another **story** soon — mouse's honor!

SOLUTIONS

Maze on pages 30–31

Puzzle on pages 56–57

Now check out this bonus
Mini Mystery story!
Join me in solving a whisker-licking-good mystery. Find clues along with me as you read. Together, we'll be super-squeaky investigators!

THE DOUBLE CROSS

A Simple Electric Razor!

What was I doing on a cruise ship? It made no sense. I don't like boats or big waves, and I almost always get **seasick** . . .

Well, it all started when my electric razor broke. One morning, I turned on my RAZOR to shave and KAPOW! Just like that, my razor practically EXPLODED in my paws, burning off half my fur!

I couldn't go to work in that state, so . . .

Oops! What a scatterbrain . . . I forgot to introduce myself. My name is Stilton, *Geronimo Stilton*. I run *The Rodent's Gazette*, the most famouse newspaper on Mouse Island.

Anyway, as I was saying, I couldn't go to work with fried fur, so I scampered off to the electronics store Wired Whiskers to buy a new razor.

"I need an electric razor," I told the salesmouse.

"Awesome!" he squeaked. "This week we're having lots of SPECIALS!"

He opened up a glass case filled with razors.

"You see this one?" he asked. "While you shave, you can listen to your favorite **music**. And it comes with a free pair of **GLOW-IN-THE-DARK** slippers!"

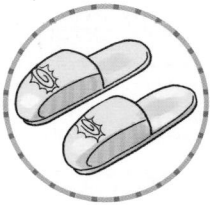

"But I don't need **slippers**," I protested.

"Then how about this one," he went on, holding up a razor that glittered. "Those are genuine diamonds!"

I almost **choked** when I saw the price.

"It comes with a free ten-year supply of spicy cheeses!" the salesmouse chirped.

"But I don't like spicy cheeses," I said.

"Well, here's one that comes with a **SOLAR-POWERED** lawn mower!" offered the salesmouse.

Finally, I couldn't take it anymore. "I just want a normal **PLASTIC** razor!" I whined.

The salesmouse looked surprised. "Why didn't you say so?" he squeaked. "Here's the one you want. It's the **Goodfur** plastic razor. It comes with a chance to **win a cruise to the Caribbean**!"

I bought the razor. As for the cruise, I never gave it a second thought.

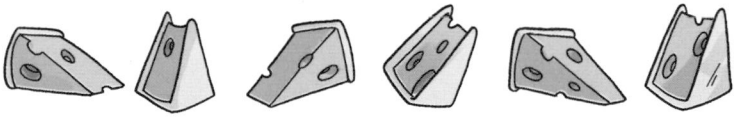

Two weeks later, a registered letter arrived for me:

CONGRATULATIONS!

You are the **lucky** winner of an all-expense-paid, **six**-day, **seven**-night cruise to the Caribbean for **four rodents**!

Brought to you by the fine rodents at Goodfur!

I sighed. As I mentioned, I'm not cruise mouse material. Just the thought of being on a boat for six days and seven nights made me feel **seasick**. But suddenly, I had an **idea**.

You Can Do It!

What if I were to invite **Petunia Pretty Paws**? Ah, what a fascinating rodent! I have had a huge crush on Petunia for the longest time. Maybe if I took her on the cruise, it wouldn't be so awful. If only I could muster the courage to call her. Oh, why am I so shy around Petunia?

you can do it! I told myself as I reached for the phone. And just then, the phone rang.

The voice on the other end of the line made my heart melt.

"**Hello, G?** It's Petunia . . ."

She was calling me!

"Hi, Netpunia, I mean, Tepunia, I mean, Petunia," I babbled. Oh, how **embarrassing**!

Luckily, Petunia didn't seem to notice. "I was hoping you could help me, G," she went on. "The government of **New Zealand** has asked me to make a documentary on the endangered **kiwi** bird. It would be an **amazing** opportunity for me."

"Congratulations!" I squeaked.

"Thanks!" Petunia

KIWI

It's the national bird of New Zealand. It has a very long beak and very small wings, but it cannot fly. It is shy and nocturnal, and it eats small insects, seeds, and worms.

gushed. "There's only one problem. Could you watch my niece Bugsy Wugsy for a few days? What do you say, G?"

I have to admit, Bugsy can really get under my fur at times. But I would never say no to Petunia, so I agreed. Then I had another idea. I could invite Bugsy, BENJAMIN, and my sister, THEA, to come on the cruise with me.

"Oh, G, you're the best!" exclaimed Petunia. "Bugsy will be so excited!"

I hung up the phone with a smile on my face. I **LOVE** making Petunia happy. Too bad she wouldn't be with me on the cruise. I could just picture it: Me, the mouse of my **dreams**, the **sunset**, the sea . . . Oh, well. Maybe next time!

EIGHT ON THE DOT

The following morning, we met at **EIGHT ON THE DOT**. Thea pulled up in her **RED** sports car with Benjamin and Bugsy in the backseat.

"Thanks for the invitation, Gerry Berry!" my sister said. "I really needed a nice vacation."

"I've never been on a **Caribbean** cruise before!" squeaked my nephew. "Thanks, Uncle Geronimo!"

Next to Benjamin, Bugsy was jumping **UP** and **DOWN** as if her fur were on fire.

"This is Sooo awesome, Uncle G!" she shrieked.

"Awesome," I agreed. Yes, a relaxing vacation *would* be awesome, if only I could forget about . . .

. . . the seasickness

. . . the big waves

. . . the too-hard or too-soft mattress

. . . the rodent-eating sharks

. . . the ship sinking

. . . the burning sun

. . . the too-cold nights

. . . the mosquitoes

. . . the pooping seagulls

. . . and, worst of all, the homesickness.

Yep, I'd *just* have to forget those things. But how?

THE *QUEEN CHEESY II*

Twenty minutes later, we reached the port of New Mouse City ready to board the cruise ship, the **Queen Cheesy II**.

Slimy Swiss Rolls! That boat was enormouse!

A rodent welcomed us to the ship.

"You must be the winners of the **Goodfur** vacation," he said. "I'm Captain Rolando Squeakando. Welcome!"

"Excuse me, Captain, how many **LIFEBOATS** are there on the **Queen Cheesy II**?" I asked.

The captain looked at me sharply. "Are you suggesting my ship is not **SAFE**, Mr. Stilton?" he asked.

Uh-oh. We hadn't even set sail and I had already insulted the mouse in charge.

"N-no, sorry," I stammered. "I just get worried."

"Well, don't worry!" Squeakando replied confidently. "We have LIFEBOATS and LIFE VESTS for every passenger!"

I must admit I was relieved. And I was glad I had put four life vests in my suitcase, just in case. Better SAFE than sorry!

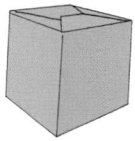

INFLATE SLOWLY... OR ELSE!

All of our cabins were on the top level, which was called the **Sky Deck**.

I found an enormouse box in my cabin. A label on the side read: "Use in case of emergency!"

How strange! The writing looked so familiar. Inside the box I found a **yellow** life vest and a **yellow** hat.

How strange! That hat reminded me of someone, but I couldn't remember who. A card attached to the vest read: **"INFLATE SLOWLY . . . OR ELSE!"**

How strange! I wondered what

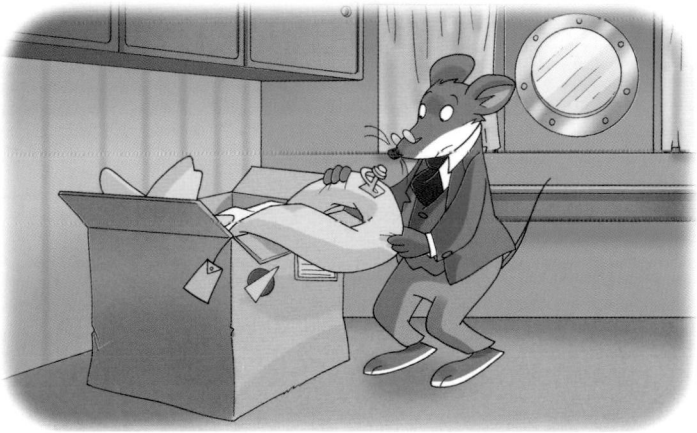

that meant. I decided there was only one way to find out. Even though it wasn't an emergency, I picked up the vest and began to INFLATE it slowly.

As I was blowing, I heard laughter.

HEE! HEE! HEE!

How strange! I was the only one in the cabin!

I kept blowing. Again, it sounded as if someone was laughing.

HEE! HEE! HEE!

My head began to pound. My fur stood on end. Who cares about getting seasick! Now I was worried about a ghost! Was my cabin haunted?

I was so nervous, I started blowing really fast.

Just then, there was a loud BOOM!

Suddenly, a mouse stood before me wearing a yellow hat and a yellow raincoat.

"How'd you like my joke, Geronimo?" he asked.

It was my friend the famouse detective **Hercule Poirat**.

"Hercule, I didn't know you were on this cruise!" I squeaked.

"Yep, I'm on the floor right below you, the Empress Deck," he said. "And I see you are traveling with the lovely Thea. Can I sit with you at dinner?"

Hercule has a crush on my sister even though she never gives him the **TIME** of day.

Still, I nodded **YES**. What else could I say?

A Cloud of Perfume

At dinnertime, the restaurant was full of mice.

I spotted Hercule over at the buffet, piling his plate **SKY-HIGH** with **delicious**-looking cheese appetizers.

Then I headed to my table, where Thea, Bugsy, and Benjamin were waiting for me. But before I reached them, I **collided** with a lady rodent who had **dropped** her evening bag.

I bent down to get it for her and was wrapped up in a **cloud of perfume**!

The smell was so strong, I got **dizzy** and crashed into a waiter carrying a pot of something **steaming**.

Oh, how **embarrassing**!

"I-I'm S-S-SORRY!" I stammered, struggling to get up.

She looked at me and I nearly fainted. Her CLEAR BLUE eyes were the color of a gorgeous summer sky and her fur was so **shiny**. What a rodent!

"Don't worry, Mr. Stilton, everyone knows great writers get distracted," she said in a voice as sweet as honey.

"You know me?" I squeaked.

She flashed me a **charming** smile. "But of course! I am Lily Lovelyfur, one of your biggest fans!" she crooned.

I **blushed**. Then I watched in a daze while she joined our table.

Lily Lovelyfur

WOULD YOU LIKE TO DANCE?

Lily Lovelyfur was mesmerizing. And, best of all, she seemed to be interested in me! I was so thrilled I hardly touched my food.

"Aren't you **hungry**, Uncle Geronimo?" Benjamin asked.

"Maybe he's SEASICK," Bugsy suggested.

Thea caught me staring at Lily Lovelyfur and grinned. "Or maybe he's got a little crush on a certain **mouse**," she teased in a singsong voice.

Before I could protest, the captain

stood up. "I'd like to welcome everyone aboard the **Queen Cheesy II**. Here's to a fabumouse voyage! And now it is our tradition to begin our cruise with some **paw-tapping** ballroom dancing!"

Within seconds, a distinguished-looking mouse appeared at our table.

"I am **Count Richie Richpaws**. May I have this dance?" he asked Thea.

"Certainly, Count," she accepted with a smile.

I wasn't surprised. My sister loves a **dashing** mouse who can dance!

"Richie Richpaws," Hercule

scoffed. "What a ridiculous name."

I was about to offer Hercule my cheddar roll to cheer him up when Miss Lovelyfur squeaked, "How about you, Mr. Stilton? Would you like to dance with me?"

Would I?! Does a mouse have WHISKERS?!

I jumped to my paws so fast I nearly fell flat on my snout.

But just as we started to dance, a mouse scampered into the ballroom.

"HELP! HELP!" she squeaked. "There's a THIEF on this ship!"

Help! Help!

A Thief in the Night!

It was Countess Von Mousenschnitz.

Sobbing, she explained how she had returned to her cabin on the Sky Deck and discovered the porthole open and her jewelry box empty!

The captain questioned all of the passengers, but he didn't uncover any CLUES.

Lily grabbed my paw. "Good thing we were together, Mr. Stilton," she squeaked. "Otherwise we might have been SUSPECTS."

I was less worried about being a suspect and more worried about being robbed myself. What if a thief stole my WHISKER TRIMMER or my GLOW-IN-THE-DARK flashlight? They weren't worth a lot of MONEY, but they were important to me.

Of course, I tried to act brave for Lily. She agreed to let me accompany her to her cabin, which was on the Empress Deck, the floor below mine.

"What a gentlemouse," she cooed.

But when we arrived, she quickly slammed the door in my snout!

How strange!

And before she slammed the door, I noticed something odd inside her cabin.

CLUE 1

Can you spot something odd in Lily Lovelyfur's cabin?

We Smell a Rat!

I headed up to the Sky Deck, still thinking about the mysterious shadow I had seen on the wall in Lily Lovelyfur's cabin. What did it mean?

I was so deep in thought I ran right into a group of rodents.

OOOF!

Luckily, it was my family.

"We were just looking for you, Uncle Geronimo," Benjamin said. "We smell a rat!"

"I think we need to investigate this THEFT," Hercule explained.

We went right to **Countess Von Mousenschnitz's** cabin. She showed us the empty **jewelry** box and the small porthole the thief had used.

Hercule pulled out a measuring tape. "This porthole is only one foot wide. It must have been a very **THIN** thief . . . or maybe a mouseling."

"I haven't seen any mouselings on board except for Bugsy and Benjamin," Thea said.

"And I haven't noticed any extremely THIN mice on board, either," Hercule added.

Suddenly, a TERRIFYING thought hit me. What if there really was a ghost on the ship? Could a ghost be responsible for the missing jewelry on the Queen Cheesy II?

I was about to squeak up when Thea looked out the porthole.

"Hey, there's a rope DANGLING out here," she said. "The thief must have used it to climb down from the Sky

Deck to the Empress Deck."

Meanwhile, Bugsy picked something up off the carpet. "Look, everyone!" she squeaked. "It's a **BLUE** contact lens!"

The countess quickly assured us the **contact lens** did not belong to her.

"Now we know something more about the **THIEF**!" Benjamin declared.

CLUE 2

What do we know now about the mysterious thief?

HUH?

The next morning on my way to breakfast I saw Lily Lovelyfur. She was wearing big, **DARK** sunglasses.

"Good morning, Miss Furrylove . . . I mean, Miss Loveydove . . . I mean . . ." I stammered.

"Good morning, Mr. Stilton!" she interrupted me. She smiled. "I **love** cruises, don't you? I'm going to the pool to get some sun."

After breakfast, I returned to my **CABIN**. On the way there, I ran into Miss Lovelyfur again.

How strange!

"I thought you were going to the **POOL**," I said.

"Oh no, Mr. Stilton," she replied. "It's too early for the **POOL**. First I need a nice breakfast."

She gave me a little wave and disappeared. I stared after her, confused. Was I losing my marbles? I decided I needed some fresh air.

I scampered to the upper deck. It really was a **beautiful** day. The sun was shining and a gentle ***wind*** was blowing. And, for once, I didn't feel seasick!

Absentmindedly, I wandered over to the pool, where I found Miss Lovelyfur sunbathing!

"Oh, Mr. Stilton, I can't wait to root for you in the **diving competition** at the pool," she squeaked. "Your friend Hercule said you had signed up."

HUH? Now I was more confused than ever!

What was going on with Miss Lovelyfur? And what diving competition was she squeaking about?

I went downstairs to ask Hercule and ran into Miss Lovelyfur . . . again!

"Time for some sun," she said.

My head was spinning.

CLUE 3

What did Geronimo Stilton see that was so strange?

I Don't Know How to Dive!

Before I could discuss things with Hercule, he grabbed my paw.

"You need an energy-packed breakfast if you're going to compete in the **diving competition**," he said. Then he made me eat:

1 cheddar quiche

2 cheese sandwiches

3 mozzarella balls

4 hot chocolates with extra cream

1 supersized banana smoothie

"But I already ate breakfast!" I protested. "And I don't even know how to dive!"

"Oh, don't be **silly**, Geronimo. You can do it!" Hercule insisted.

Then he dragged me to his cabin and made me change into a bright-yellow bathing suit with BANANAS all over it. I looked ridiculous! **How embarrassing!**

Don't Look Down!

All of the passengers had gathered on the pool deck to watch the competition.

The captain spoke from a megaphone:

"Ladies and gentlemice, welcome to the Queen Cheesy II's fabumouse diving competition!"

I **trembled** with fear. The diving board was so **HIGH**! I wondered if I would even be able to make it up the ladder! I thought about ***running*** away.

But when I looked around, I saw Benjamin, Bugsy, Thea, and even **Count Richie Richpaws** all cheering me on.

What could I do? I couldn't disappoint everyone. When it was my turn, I slowly began CLIMBING up the ladder.

Holey cheese! I was so dizzy from the HEIGHT!

I glanced down and spotted Lily Lovelyfur. She blew me a **kiss**! Now I felt even **dizzier**!

"Don't look down!" I heard Hercule shout from below.

Don't look down! I thought to myself as I walked to the edge of the board.

Little did I know, Hercule had put a banana peel on the diving board! Suddenly, I slipped, **BOUNCED**, did three **spectacular** somersaults, and fell snoutfirst into the water.

It was a *perfect* dive!

When I emerged from the water, everyone was applauding!

I had **WON**!

EYES LIKE GREEN EMERALDS!

That night, there was an AWARDS CEREMONY.

"I told you you could do it!" Hercule said, shaking my paw until I felt like it would fall off.

"You could have killed me with that BANANA PEEL," I muttered.

But Hercule just winked.

Meanwhile, Benjamin, Bugsy, Thea, and Count Richpaws all congratulated me.

"Way to go, Uncle Geronimo!" my nephew squeaked.

"I thought you'd **CRACK** your head

open like a nut, Uncle G!" Bugsy marveled.

"It would be my **pleasure** if you would join me tonight at my table, Mr. Stilton," the count declared. "And why don't you ask your friend Miss Lovelyfur to join us, too?"

Suddenly, Lily appeared by my side. Before I could even squeak a word, she said, "I would **love** to join you, Mr. Stilton. Who wouldn't want to have dinner with such a talented ATHLETE?!"

She lowered her glasses and winked at me. Then she scampered off.

I stood there, **dazzled** by her

eyes, which sparkled like **green emeralds**!

A funny feeling came over me. There was something different about Miss Lovelyfur, but I just couldn't put my paw on it. Did she have a new **fur-style**? Was she wearing a different shade of **lipstick**?

It was all so confusing. I was still

thinking about Lily when the count cleared his throat.

"See you at dinner, Mr. Stilton. And now, I promised your sister I would show her one of my most **priceless** collections."

After they left, Benjamin **TUGGED** on my sleeve. "Uncle Geronimo, did you notice something different about Miss Lovelyfur?" he squeaked. "Something about her eyes?"

Just then it **hit** me! Now I knew exactly what was different!

CLUE 4

What do Benjamin and Geronimo realize is different about Lily Lovelyfur?

SORRY I'M LATE!

At dinner, we all sat at the count's table. The waiters began serving our meal, but still there was no SIGN of Lily. Was she sick? Was it something I said?

But then, suddenly, Lily appeared. Once again, I was **dazzled** by her eyes. But this time they were **BLUE** again!

How strange! This afternoon I was sure her eyes had been **green**. I made a mental note to make an appointment with my eye doctor, Dr. Bifocals, when I

got home. Maybe I was **colorblind**!

"Good evening, everyone. Sorry I'm late!" Miss Lovelyfur apologized. "I was feeling a little **SEASICK**. I don't like cruises very much."

Huh? Now I was really confused. That didn't make sense.

But before I had a chance to ask, **THREE** things happened. First, Hercule accidentally **squeezed** lemon juice in my eye. Next, he ladled a spoonful of **boiling** soup on my paw by mistake. And, finally, he **HIT ME** in the snout with a piece of cake! **I WAS A MESS!**

I was hoping no one had noticed when the count suggested we all go

Hercule sprayed lemon juice in my eye.

He spilled boiling soup on my paw.

Then he flung a piece of cake in my snout.

outside to look at the STARS.

"I need to grab something from my cabin, then I'll meet you," he said.

The rest of us headed up to the deck. It was a beautiful night. The sea was calm, there was a cool breeze, and the stars twinkled overhead.

The smell of Lily's perfume made me smile.

Still, I couldn't stop thinking about what she had said. . . .

CLUE 5

What did Lily say that didn't make any sense?

What a beautiful sky!
Wow!

THIEF! THIEF!

I was still thinking about Lily when suddenly we heard a mouse squeaking in the ballroom.

"**THIEF! THIEF!** My gold watches are gone!"

We dashed inside and discovered the count in a **RAGE**.

"It was you!" he squeaked, pointing at Thea. "I showed you my precious collection of gold watches, and then you stole them!"

Thea **narrowed** her eyes. Uh-oh. I

could tell she was ANGRIER than a lab rat stuck in a maze!

"How dare you accuse me!" she squeaked, her eyes **flashing**.

One thing you should know about Thea is that she is one **TOUGH** mouse. Her paws were **balled** into fists. She

looked like she wanted to **SHOUT** right back at Count Richie.

Luckily, the **captain** arrived.

"Calm down, everyone," he said, holding up a paw. "Tell me what happened . . ."

Before the count could explain, my sister blurted out the whole story. I confirmed that Thea had been with us the whole time, so she couldn't be the **THIEF**. The captain agreed.

"Don't worry," he said. "We will **MONITOR** the cabins day and night until we catch the thief.

You have my **WORD**!"

We left the ballroom and returned to our cabins for the night. Before I reached mine, though, I decided to do the gentlemousely thing and walk Lily back to her cabin.

She thanked me with a **mesmerizing** smile. Ah, what a mouse. "I'm so glad I was with you, Mr. Stilton," she squeaked. "I would hate it if anyone thought we were **suspects**."

I left her at her door and returned to my cabin. Later, I was just drifting off to sleep when there was a knock at my door.

KNOCK! KNOCK! KNOCK!

ARE YOU SURE?

I opened the door. Hercule stood in front of me, his paws on his hips.

"What's the matter with you, Geronimo?" he scolded. "Don't you know how to treat a LaDy?"

Huh? What was he squeaking about?

"A true gentlemouse would have walked his date home," he explained. "I just left Miss Lovelyfur in front of her cabin after you abandoned her."

Now I was completely confused. I had just said good night to Lily a few minutes ago . . .

Hercule explained that he was walking back to his cabin when he spotted Lily. She said she had been walking **down** the stairs to her cabin when she'd **SLIPPED** and fallen.

"Luckily, she grabbed on to a rope dangling from the Sky Deck. Then I rescued her," Hercule squeaked proudly.

I frowned. Hercule's story didn't make any **sense**.

"Are you sure it was her?" I squeaked.

"Of course," Hercule insisted. "I even carried her **HEAVY** backpack. By the way, have you noticed that she has one green eye and one **BLUE** eye?"

Empress
113

HOLEY SWISS CHEESE!

I closed my eyes and pictured Lily. The first day I met her, her eyes had been clear BLUE, like a summer sky. But then at the awards ceremony, her eyes were the color of sparkling green emeralds. What was going on?

Later that night, we gathered in Thea's cabin to see if we could solve the mystery.

"When Count Richpaws was meeting with the captain, we checked out his cabin," Benjamin said. "We found a ROPE tied outside his window, and a

BLUE contact lens on the floor."

"Just like the contact I found on the floor in the countess's cabin!" Bugsy exclaimed.

Two different-colored eyes? A blue contact lens?

"**Holey Swiss cheese!**" I squeaked. "I think I've figured it out!"

CLUE 6

What did Geronimo figure out?

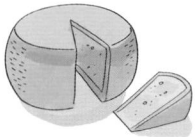

To Catch a Thief

After I explained my suspicions to everyone, Hercule came up with a plan to catch the **THIEF**. Too bad it involved little old me. I was a nervous wreck!

The next day, we set the plan in motion. First, I invited Miss Lovelyfur to lunch. Then I told her about my precious CHEESE RIND collection from the 1700s.

"I always carry it with me," I explained. "It's too VALUABLE to leave at home. I hid it in my cabin. I just hope it's safe with all of these THEFTS!"

Lily's blue eyes FLASHED with excitement. "Oh, I'm sure it's safe," she said soothingly.

THE TRAP

That **evening**, everyone on the ship gathered in the ballroom. The captain announced a big **SURPRISE**.

"One of our passengers has decided to put up a very PRECIOUS object for auction," he said. "The proceeds will go to benefit needy mice in New Mouse City!"

"A PRECIOUS object . . . How interesting," Miss Lovelyfur commented. "I wonder what it is. And who could the passenger be?"

I smiled at her. "It's me!" I said.

"You remember my CHEESE collection?" I explained. "Well, I decided to donate it for a good cause."

At my news, Lily's fur turned as pale as a slice of mozzarella. Suddenly, she headed for the door.

"Be right back," she mumbled.

But she didn't get far. Just then, Benjamin, Bugsy, Thea, and Hercule arrived. Hercule was escorting a mouse who looked EXACTLY like Lily! Yep, the two mice were identical except for one thing: the Lily standing next to me had BLUE eyes. And the Lily with Hercule had green eyes!

TWIN THIEVES

"**WHAT IS GOING ON HERE?!**" the captain demanded.

"Well, Captain," Hercule squeaked, "you don't have to worry about any more thefts, because here is your thief. Well, actually, your **two** thieves."

I was about to confront the Lily beside me, but I never got the chance. Two seconds later, she

fainted.

Two thieves?!

It turned out that the thieves were actually twins named Samantha and Sasha Stickypaws. They had used colored contact lenses to trick everyone on the ship into thinking they were **one** mouse.

Samantha was a registered passenger, but Sasha had snuck aboard the ship.

During the day, the two mice dressed alike so that they could walk around the boat at the same time. While Samantha looked for rich passengers on

the **POOL** deck, Sasha searched the cabins below.

At night, one sister **broke** into the cabins, stealing PRECIOUS items. Meanwhile, the other sister made sure

SAMANTHA STICKYPAWS BROKE INTO CABINS.

SASHA STICKYPAWS DANCED WITH GERONIMO.

everyone saw her dining and dancing with me so no one would **suspect** her.

When Hercule was done explaining everything, I felt a little **foolish**. After all, the Stickypaws twins had set me up! I should have known there was something **STRANGE** about Lily Lovelyfur. Right then and there, I promised myself I'd never again get sidetracked by a fascinating female rodent. But that got me thinking about **Petunia Pretty Paws**. She was kind, smart, and completely **fascinating**. I sighed. Something told me I might have a little **trouble** keeping that promise.

SMOOTH SAILING!

I was still thinking about Petunia as I watched the Stickypaws twins being led away. Of course, the captain had them return all of the PRECIOUS jewels they had stolen.

Count Richie Richpaws apologized to Thea for accusing her of stealing his gold watch collection. Then he decided to give the whole collection away in the charity auction. Soon, lots of other passengers decided to donate items to the auction. It was an enormouse success!

I was so happy we were making money for my favorite charity, I almost forgot all about the THIEVES and my seasickness. In fact, I had a feeling that the rest of the cruise would be . . .

YOU'RE THE INVESTIGATOR!

DID YOU FIGURE OUT THE CLUES?

1 Look at the illustration on page 144. Can you spot something odd in Lily Lovelyfur's cabin?
There is a shadow on the wall.

2 What do we know now about the mysterious thief?
That he/she wears contact lenses.

3 What did Geronimo Stilton see that was so strange?
He saw Miss Lovelyfur appear in different places at almost the same time. First she said she was going to the pool, then she said she was heading to breakfast.

4 What do Benjamin and Geronimo realize is different about Lily Lovelyfur?
Her eye color changed from blue to green.

5 What did Lily say that didn't make any sense?
She said that she sufferred from seasickness. But in the morning, she had said she loved cruises.

6 What did Geronimo figure out?
That the blue contact lenses found in the two cabins explained the different color of Lily's eyes. They also proved she had been in both the countess's and the count's cabins.

HOW MANY QUESTIONS DID YOU ANSWER CORRECTLY?

ALL 6 CORRECT: You are a **SUPER-SQUEAKY INVESTIGATOR!**

FROM 3 TO 5 CORRECT: You are a **SUPER INVESTIGATOR!** You'll get that added squeak soon!

LESS THAN 3 CORRECT: You are a **GOOD INVESTIGATOR!** Keep practicing to get super-squeaky!

Farewell until the next mystery!

Geronimo Stilton

GERONIMO'S JOKES

Q **Why was the spider on the computer?**

A To make a *web*site!

Q **Why did it take the sailor mouse so long to learn the alphabet?**

A He spent years at *C*!

Q **Why did the vampire have no friends?**

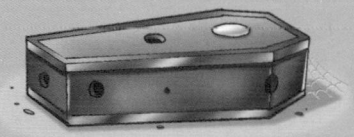

A Because he was a pain in the neck!

Q **What game did the cat like to play with the mouse?**

A Catch!

Q What do you get from a pampered cow?

A Spoiled milk!

Q Why are fish so smart?

A Because they live in schools!

Q Why can't a leopard hide?

A Because she's always spotted!

Q What kind of bow can't be tied?

A A rainbow!

Q **Why couldn't the mouse open the piano?**

A The keys were inside!

Q **What did one eye say to the other?**

A "Between you and me, something smells!"

Q **What was the cat's favorite color?**

A *Purr*-ple!

Q **What is a pirate's favorite subject in school?**

A *Arrrrt*!

Q **Why did the bee go to the doctor?**

A Because she had hives!

Q **Why was the math homework sad?**

A It had so many problems!

Q **What have heads and tails but no legs?**

A Coins!

Q **What did one campfire say to the other?**

A "Will you go out tonight?"

Be sure to read all my fabumouse adventures!

#1 Lost Treasure of the Emerald Eye

#2 The Curse of the Cheese Pyramid

#3 Cat and Mouse in a Haunted House

#4 I'm Too Fond of My Fur!

#5 Four Mice Deep in the Jungle

#6 Paws Off, Cheddarface!

#7 Red Pizzas for a Blue Count

#8 Attack of the Bandit Cats

#9 A Fabumouse Vacation for Geronimo

#10 All Because of a Cup of Coffee

#11 It's Halloween, You 'Fraidy Mouse!

#12 Merry Christmas, Geronimo!

#13 The Phantom of the Subway

#14 The Temple of the Ruby of Fire

#15 The Mona Mousa Code

#16 A Cheese-Colored Camper

#17 Watch Your Whiskers, Stilton!

#18 Shipwreck on the Pirate Islands

#19 My Name Is Stilton, Geronimo Stilton

#20 Surf's Up, Geronimo!

#21 The Wild, Wild West

#22 The Secret of Cacklefur Castle

A Christmas Tale

#23 Valentine's Day Disaster

#24 Field Trip to Niagara Falls

#25 The Search for Sunken Treasure

#26 The Mummy with No Name

#27 The Christmas Toy Factory

#28 Wedding Crasher

#29 Down and Out Down Under

#30 The Mouse Island Marathon

#31 The Mysterious Cheese Thief

Christmas Catastrophe

#32 Valley of the Giant Skeletons

#33 Geronimo and the Gold Medal Mystery

#34 Geronimo Stilton, Secret Agent

#35 A Very Merry Christmas

#36 Geronimo's Valentine

#37 The Race Across America

#38 A Fabumouse School Adventure

#39 Singing Sensation

#40 The Karate Mouse

#41 Mighty Mount Kilimanjaro

#42 The Peculiar Pumpkin Thief

#43 I'm Not a Supermouse!

#44 The Giant Diamond Robbery

#45 Save the White Whale!

#46 The Haunted Castle

#47 Run for the Hills, Geronimo!

#48 The Mystery in Venice

#49 The Way of the Samurai

#50 This Hotel Is Haunted!

#51 The Enormouse Pearl Heist

#52 Mouse in Space!

#53 Rumble in the Jungle

#54 Get into Gear, Stilton!

#55 The Golden Statue Plot

#56 Flight of the Red Bandit

The Hunt for the Golden Book

#57 The Stinky Cheese Vacation

#58 The Super Chef Contest

#59 Welcome to Moldy Manor

The Hunt for the Curious Cheese

#60 The Treasure of Easter Island

#61 Mouse House Hunter

#62 Mouse Overboard!

The Hunt for the Secret Papyrus

#63 The Cheese Experiment

#64 Magical Mission

#65 Bollywood Burglary

The Hunt for the Hundredth Key

Up next:

#66 Operation: Secret Recipe

Join me and my friends as we travel through time in these very special editions!

THE JOURNEY THROUGH TIME

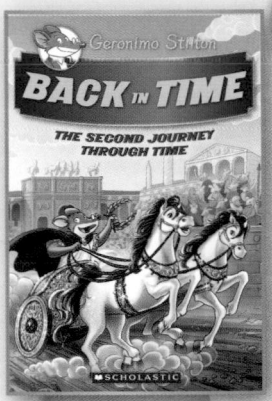

BACK IN TIME:
THE SECOND JOURNEY THROUGH TIME

THE RACE AGAINST TIME:
THE THIRD JOURNEY THROUGH TIME

LOST IN TIME:
THE FOURTH JOURNEY THROUGH TIME

MEET
Geronimo Stiltonord

He is a mouseking – the Geronimo Stilton of the ancient far north! He lives with his brawny and brave clan in the village of Mouseborg. From sailing frozen waters to facing fiery dragons, every day is an adventure for the micekings!

#1 Attack of the Dragons

#2 The Famouse Fjord Race

#3 Pull the Dragon's Tooth!

#4 Stay Strong, Geronimo!

#5 The Mysterious Message

Don't miss any of my adventures in the Kingdom of Fantasy!

The Kingdom of Fantasy

The Quest for Paradise:
The Return to the Kingdom of Fantasy

The Amazing Voyage:
The Third Adventure in the Kingdom of Fantasy

The Dragon Prophecy:
The Fourth Adventure in the Kingdom of Fantasy

The Volcano of Fire:
The Fifth Adventure in the Kingdom of Fantasy

The Search for Treasure:
The Sixth Adventure in the Kingdom of Fantasy

The Enchanted Charms:
The Seventh Adventure in the Kingdom of Fantasy

The Phoenix of Destiny:
An Epic Kingdom of Fantasy Adventure

The Hour of Magic:
The Eighth Adventure in the Kingdom of Fantasy

The Wizard's Wand:
The Ninth Adventure in the Kingdom of Fantasy

Don't miss any of these exciting Thea Sisters adventures!

Thea Stilton and the Dragon's Code

Thea Stilton and the Mountain of Fire

Thea Stilton and the Ghost of the Shipwreck

Thea Stilton and the Secret City

Thea Stilton and the Mystery in Paris

Thea Stilton and the Cherry Blossom Adventure

Thea Stilton and the Star Castaways

Thea Stilton: Big Trouble in the Big Apple

Thea Stilton and the Ice Treasure

Thea Stilton and the Secret of the Old Castle

Thea Stilton and the Blue Scarab Hunt

Thea Stilton and the Prince's Emerald

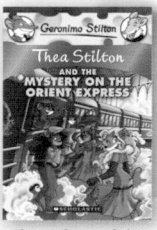

Thea Stilton and the Mystery on the Orient Express

Thea Stilton and the Dancing Shadows

Thea Stilton and the Legend of the Fire Flowers

Thea Stilton and the Spanish Dance Mission

Thea Stilton and the Journey to the Lion's Den

Thea Stilton and the Great Tulip Heist

Thea Stilton and the Chocolate Sabotage

Thea Stilton and the Missing Myth

Thea Stilton and the Lost Letters

Thea Stilton and the Tropical Treasure

Thea Stilton and the Hollywood Hoax

Thea Stilton and the Madagascar Madness

Meet Geronimo Stiltonix

He is a spacemouse — the Geronimo Stilton of a parallel universe! He is captain of the spaceship *MouseStar 1*. While flying through the cosmos, he visits distant planets and meets crazy aliens. His adventures are out of this world!

#1 Alien Escape

#2 You're Mine, Captain!

#3 Ice Planet Adventure

#4 The Galactic Goal

#5 Rescue Rebellion

#6 The Underwater Planet

#7 Beware! Space Junk!

#8 Away in a Star Sled

#9 Slurp Monster Showdown

#10 Pirate Spacecat Attack

Meet GERONIMO STILTONOOT

He is a cavemouse — Geronimo Stilton's ancient ancestor! He runs the stone newspaper in the prehistoric village of Old Mouse City. From dealing with dinosaurs to dodging meteorites, his life in the Stone Age is full of adventure!

#1 The Stone of Fire

#2 Watch Your Tail!

#3 Help, I'm in Hot Lava!

#4 The Fast and the Frozen

#5 The Great Mouse Race

#6 Don't Wake the Dinosaur!

#7 I'm a Scaredy-Mouse!

#8 Surfing for Secrets

#9 Get the Scoop, Geronimo!

#10 My Autosaurus Will Win!

#11 Sea Monster Surprise

#12 Paws Off the Pearl!

#13 The Smelly Search

#14 Shoo, Caveflies!

About the Author

Born in New Mouse City, Mouse Island, **Geronimo Stilton** is Rattus Emeritus of Mousomorphic Literature and of Neo-Ratonic Comparative Philosophy. For the past twenty years, he has been running *The Rodent's Gazette*, New Mouse City's most widely read daily newspaper.

Stilton was awarded the Ratitzer Prize for his scoops on *The Curse of the Cheese Pyramid* and *The Search for Sunken Treasure*. He has also received the Andersen 2000 Prize for Personality of the Year. One of his bestsellers won the 2002 eBook Award for world's best ratlings' electronic book. His works have been published all over the globe.

In his spare time, Mr. Stilton collects antique cheese rinds and plays golf. But what he most enjoys is telling stories to his nephew Benjamin.

6
5
4
3
2
1
1. Main entrance
2. Printing presses (where the books and newspaper are printed)
3. Accounts department
4. Editorial room (where the editors, illustrators, and designers work)
5. Geronimo Stilton's office
6. Helicopter landing pad
THE RODENT'S GAZETTE

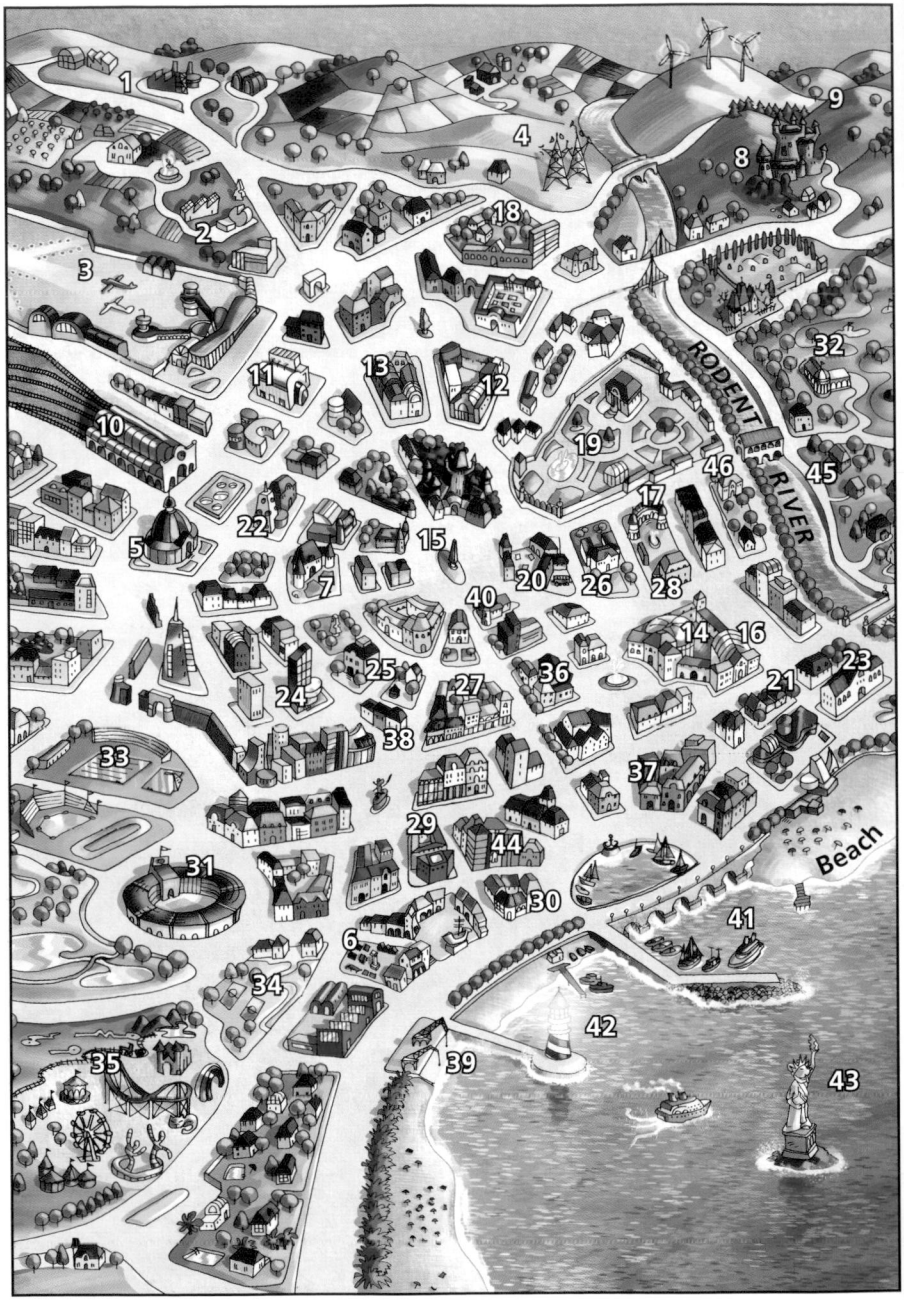
1
2
3
4
5
6
7
8
9
10
11
12
13
14
15
16
17
18
19
20
21
22
23
24
25
26
27
28
29
30
31
32
33
34
35
36
37
38
39
40
41
42
43
44
45
46
RODENT RIVER
Beach

Map of New Mouse City

1. Industrial Zone
2. Cheese Factories
3. Angorat International Airport
4. WRAT Radio and Television Station
5. Cheese Market
6. Fish Market
7. Town Hall
8. Snotnose Castle
9. The Seven Hills of Mouse Island
10. Mouse Central Station
11. Trade Center
12. Movie Theater
13. Gym
14. Catnegie Hall
15. Singing Stone Plaza
16. The Gouda Theater
17. Grand Hotel
18. Mouse General Hospital
19. Botanical Gardens
20. Cheap Junk for Less (Trap's store)
21. Aunt Sweetfur and Benjamin's House
22. Mouseum of Modern Art
23. University and Library
24. *The Daily Rat*
25. *The Rodent's Gazette*
26. Trap's House
27. Fashion District
28. The Mouse House Restaurant
29. Environmental Protection Center
30. Harbor Office
31. Mousidon Square Garden
32. Golf Course
33. Swimming Pool
34. Tennis Courts
35. Curlyfur Island Amousement Park
36. Geronimo's House
37. Historic District
38. Public Library
39. Shipyard
40. Thea's House
41. New Mouse Harbor
42. Luna Lighthouse
43. The Statue of Liberty
44. Hercule Poirat's Office
45. Petunia Pretty Paws's House
46. Grandfather William's House

This way to the Rodent Straits
Brigand's Isle
Tomcat Island
Pirate Ship of Cats
Hamster Islands
Blue Dolphin Bay
Cat's Claw Bay
Panther Archipelago
Coral Reefs
Swissville
This way to the Mousific Ocean
Stray Cat Harbor
Cheddarton
Mouseport
San Mouscisco
This way to the Ratlantic Ocean
New Mouse City
Mousefort Beach
Furflung Island
This way to the Sea of Mice
N
W
E
S
MOUSE ISLAND
1
2
3
4
5
6
7
8
9
10
11
12
13
14
15
16
17
18
19
20
21
22
23
24
25
26
27
28
29
30
31
32
33
34
35
36
37

Map of Mouse Island

1. Big Ice Lake
2. Frozen Fur Peak
3. Slipperyslopes Glacier
4. Coldcreeps Peak
5. Ratzikistan
6. Transratania
7. Mount Vamp
8. Roastedrat Volcano
9. Brimstone Lake
10. Poopedcat Pass
11. Stinko Peak
12. Dark Forest
13. Vain Vampires Valley
14. Goose Bumps Gorge
15. The Shadow Line Pass
16. Penny Pincher Castle
17. Nature Reserve Park
18. Las Ratayas Marinas
19. Fossil Forest
20. Lake Lake
21. Lake Lakelake
22. Lake Lakelakelake
23. Cheddar Crag
24. Cannycat Castle
25. Valley of the Giant Sequoia
26. Cheddar Springs
27. Sulfurous Swamp
28. Old Reliable Geyser
29. Vole Vale
30. Ravingrat Ravine
31. Gnat Marshes
32. Munster Highlands
33. Mousehara Desert
34. Oasis of the Sweaty Camel
35. Cabbagehead Hill
36. Rattytrap Jungle
37. Rio Mosquito

Dear mouse friends,
Thanks for reading, and farewell
till the next book.
It'll be another whisker-licking-good
adventure, and that's a promise!

Geronimo Stilton